I Know an Old Lady Who Swallowed a Fly

Retold and Illustrated by
Nadine Bernard Westcott

Little, Brown and Company
BOSTON   NEW YORK   LONDON

PB: 25 24 23 22

Library of Congress Cataloging in Publication Data

Westcott, Nadine Bernard.
  I know an old lady who swallowed a fly.

  A retelling of the Little old lady who swallowed a fly.

  SUMMARY: A cumulative rhyme in which the solution proves worse than the predicament when an old lady swallows a fly.
  1. Folk-songs, English. [1. Nonsense verses. 2. Folk songs, English] I. Little old lady who swallowed a fly. II. Title.
PZ8.3.W4998Iac   811'.5'4   79-24728

ISBN 0-316-93127-6 pbk.

SC

PRINTED IN HONG KONG

For my husband, Bill,
who makes all things possible

I know an old lady who swallowed a fly,

I don't know why she swallowed a fly,

Perhaps she'll die.

I know an old lady who swallowed a spider

That wiggled and jiggled and tickled inside her.

She swallowed the spider to catch the fly,
I don't know why she swallowed the fly,

Perhaps she'll die.

I know an old lady who swallowed a bird,
How absurd to swallow a bird!

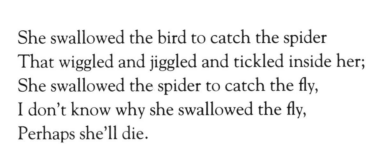

She swallowed the bird to catch the spider
That wiggled and jiggled and tickled inside her;
She swallowed the spider to catch the fly,
I don't know why she swallowed the fly,
Perhaps she'll die.

I know an old lady who swallowed a cat,
Think of that, she swallowed a cat!

She swallowed the cat to catch the bird,

She swallowed the bird to catch the spider
That wiggled and jiggled and tickled inside her;
She swallowed the spider to catch the fly,
I don't know why she swallowed the fly,
Perhaps she'll die.

I know an old lady who swallowed a dog,
Oh, what a hog to swallow a dog!

She swallowed the dog to catch the cat,
She swallowed the cat to catch the bird,

She swallowed the bird to catch the spider
That wiggled and jiggled and tickled inside her;
She swallowed the spider to catch the fly,
I don't know why she swallowed the fly,
Perhaps she'll die.

I know an old lady who swallowed a goat,

Popped open her throat and swallowed a goat.

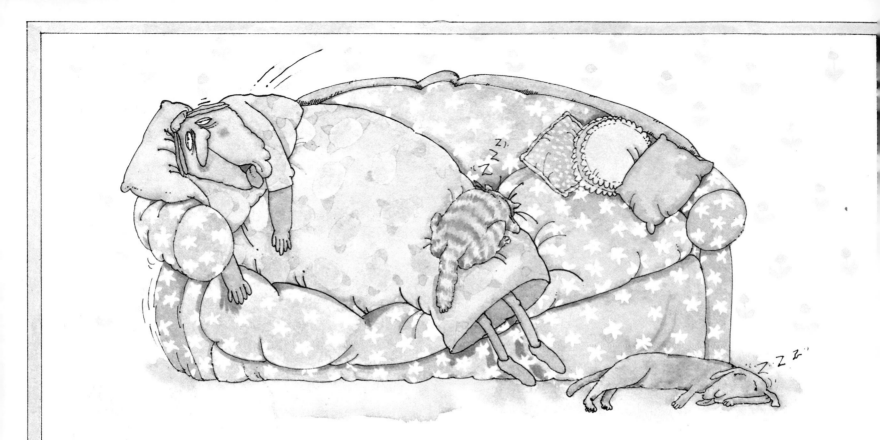

She swallowed the goat to catch the dog,
She swallowed the dog to catch the cat,
She swallowed the cat to catch the bird,
She swallowed the bird to catch the spider
That wiggled and jiggled and tickled inside her;
She swallowed the spider to catch the fly,

I don't know why she swallowed the fly,
Perhaps she'll die.

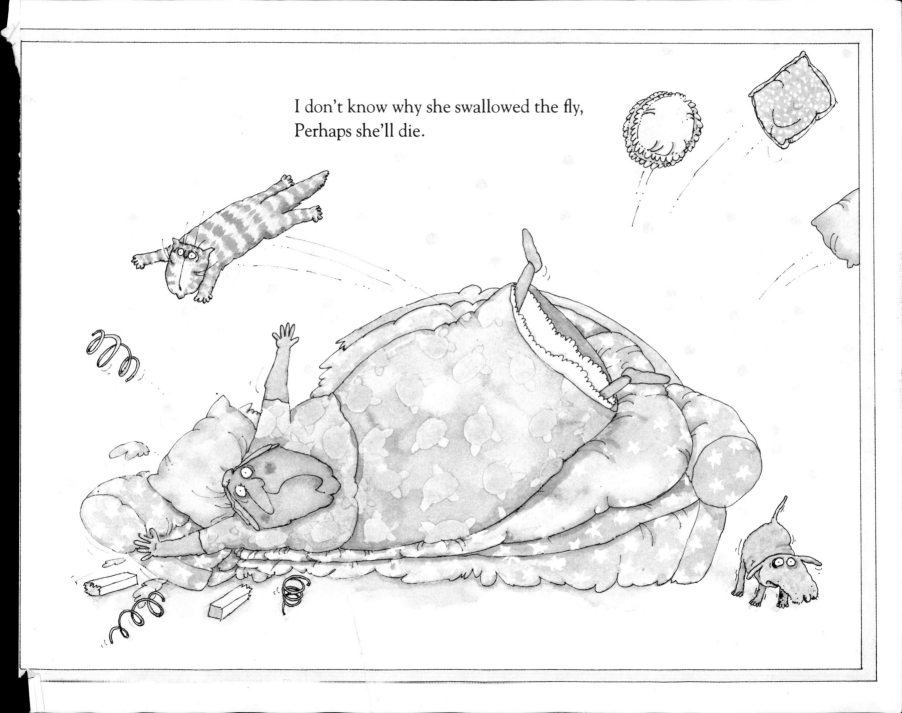

I know an old lady who swallowed a cow,

Don't ask how she swallowed a cow.

She swallowed the cow to catch the goat,
She swallowed the goat to catch the dog,
She swallowed the dog to catch the cat,
She swallowed the cat to catch the bird,
She swallowed the bird to catch the spider
That wiggled and jiggled and tickled inside her;
She swallowed the spider to catch the fly,

I don't know why she swallowed the fly,
Perhaps she'll die.

I know an old lady who swallowed a horse,

She died, of course!